Praise for *The Book of Morfeo* and Stefano Benni

"In *The Book of Morfeo*, Benni delivers a vibrant condemnation of the power of the pharmaceutical companies and their pursuit of profit by flooding the market with addictive products." *Cultura e Spettacolo Magazine*

"Benni's visionary imagination creates a powerful, poignant book that tells a story that is part fairy tale, part tragedy, part dream, and part delirium. Benni denounces the 'chemical oppression' of the pharmaceutical industry which becomes a universal metaphor for unjust oppression throughout the world." *La Repubblica*

"The best Benni in recent years." *RAI News*

"*The Book of Morfeo* offers salvation at the edge of the abyss." *La Stampa*

"A varied universe, narrated in surreal colors, that takes us by the hand and leads us to an unexpected conclusion." *L'almanacco della Scienza*

"Stefano Benni loves to play with language, his books delight in inventive or specialist vocabulary. Irresistible neologisms and freewheeling imagery are drafted in from the Alamo to the Zambezi, from the desert fox to the sea cucumber. You never know what's coming next." *The Sunday Telegraph*

"Benni is sly and spiky in his satire." *Publishers Weekly*

THE BOOK OF MORFEO
By Stefano Benni

(Originally published as
La traccia dell'angelo)

Kazabo Publishing

Translation © 2021 Kazabo Publishing
© 2011 Sellerio Editore, Palermo

Garamond MT Std 12/14/20

ISBN: 978-1-948104-21-0

Kazabo books are available at special
discounts when purchased in bulk or by
book clubs. Special editions of many of our
books can also be created for promotional
and educational use. Please visit us at
kazabo.com for more information.

Foreword

Stefano Benni, born in Bologna in 1947, is something of an artistic polymath. He's a journalist, director, performer, playwright, and lyricist as well as an artistic consultant for one of the longest-running jazz festivals in Italy. His work has been released on multiple albums and he regularly tours. But these achievements pale in comparison to his literary output.

Benni has published over 20 novels and his books have been translated into 32 languages. But he is most popular in his native Italy where, as one critic observed, he is "treated more like a rock star than a writer."

Perhaps most impressive, however, is that Benni has managed to combine mass-market popularity with literary heft. His unique blend of magical realism, satire, and comedy is now regarded in Italy as its own literary style: "Benniano."

Stefano Benni's books are always involving tales on their own terms. Yet they are also, inevitably, "about" something. In fact, Benni's books are about many things. Benni has a way of treating metaphors like onions. One interpretation may be both perfectly satisfying and perfectly correct. And yet, there is a fresh interpretation waiting just below the surface which reflects the story in a whole new light. That's one of the trademarks of the Benniano style. A comic satire on some current event or social trend is often, at a deeper level, a meditation on a human universal. Sometimes his work seems casual, almost stream-of-consciousness, yet there is always a complex and coherent underlying structure. Stefano Benni is one of those rare authors whose works become more engaging on a second – or third – reading rather than less. He would have made an excellent Greek playwright.

God is perfect, so He has nothing to strive for. Man does.

The only joy is cheating death. The only act both human and divine is healing.

Part One

Christmas, 1955

The only way to not fear Death is not to think about her, not to listen to her. To turn your back on her, even though she is everywhere, and you can't turn your back on what is everywhere. Can you turn your back on the desert? One of the mysteries of Death is this lunacy of ours: struggling not to fear her.

When Little Morfeo was eight years old, he didn't believe in Death. She was a topic reserved for adults, a topic that made them loquacious and confused. They didn't love her, but they spoke of her, constantly, obsessively, as if she were a real person who was now absent.

Perhaps a hateful, petty, evil, spiteful person, but one who had walked among them.

So Morfeo enjoyed a wonderful childhood without Death, where Death is hiding, silent, invisible. She stays hidden, like the skull beneath the skin of your face, or a smashed cat on the road, a comical steak. But the grin on the skull remains, unvaried over the centuries, inside the coffins, the ossuaries, the mass graves. Teeth, teeth surviving far longer than our beautiful eyes, our charming voices. When Death speaks to you with her indestructible smile and touches your shoulder, your childhood is over.

It was the year... but who cares about the date? It was an old Christmas in the pre-cellular Paleozoic age, when a pine tree in your living room was not ecological genocide. And it was snowing like it used to do in classic movies. Of course, it also snows nowadays, but it does it without any artistic merit, and snow is now a news headline, not a natural result of the changing seasons.

Morfeo was spending that happy day at his grandparents' house, just as the family had done for years. It was a small villa in the hills, set among poplars and cypress trees, a cozy oasis where running water and electricity had arrived just that year and with them, radiators and light bulbs. It was Morfeo's first amazing Christmas without oil lamps and no need for a fireplace. But the fireplace was lit, as required by tradition, and there were candles, simple Franciscan sisters replacing the more mundane light bulbs.

"I like the candlelight," the boy mused, sitting under a window that framed a hilly, snowy landscape, eating peanuts and dried figs, and inhaling the forest smell of the Christmas tree, green umbrella of the winter cold, pagan totem of the western aboriginals. He loved the odor of pine needles and candles leaking drops of hot snow. While crushing nut sarcophagi, he contemplated the chocolate Santa cadavers dangling from the tree branches, and the silver festoons, and the lights, flashing in a multiplicity of patterns, a miracle of modern times. Not to mention the Christmas tree balls, as precious as jewelry, chosen every year, two at a time, at the Christmas Market of the Saint Lucia Fair; and at the top of all that wonder, shining like a scepter, a silver angel with open wings.

He studied the wrapped gifts under the tree. They were a tenth of the number you'd find today but were not 90% useless, wasted words of love. Already a little sleepy, Morfeo was trying to figure out which one of those packages contained, in addition to the mandatory nougat, his personal gift: Swoppets, soldiers with interchangeable parts and a rare brand of toy, a precious gift in a way that Gormiti, Winx or Pokemon never were.

How many of the little soldiers would he receive? Perhaps three, perhaps four, the prone rifleman, the menacing Native American, already on the road to extinction, the black-hatted gunman posing as if for a photograph, perhaps an excellent Apache warrior on horseback.

4

He surveyed the room. There was his sister, who was stuffing her mouth with nougat, her braces cracking like a machine gun.

His grandfather, working on his third serving of tortellini, which he consumed slowly and relentlessly using his single remaining tooth while the rest of the family still at the table was already eating fruit.

His mother with her narrow, jaundiced face and exaggerated cheekbones, still thin and pained as if the hunger of the war had never left her.

His father, Giobbe, sitting in front of the fireplace and smoking cheap, damp cigarettes until only the filter was left.

Now his father, he was someone who thought about Death.

Out of his battalion of real soldiers, half were dead and he knew them all. Coughing he would repeat, "Dear Morfeo, you're lucky, you'll never have to go to war. You can't imagine how many awful things you'll be spared. . ." And then he talked of holes in bellies, and agony, and of a German dangling from a tree branch.

In his head, Morfeo pictured that lousy Kraut dangling like one of the chocolate Santas on the tree.

His Grandmother Adele, an ancient turtle, wrapped in a camphor-smelling shawl, gazing at everyone with both hatred and benevolence.

She was like two different people, a centenarian Minotaur: the top half sweet, the lower half mean, and impaled on a wheelchair.

His mother stood up and announced, "We have a surprise! Uncle Pupo sent us a wonderful *cicerchiata* cake, all the way from Abruzzo!" The reaction to this announcement was instant and unanimous. "Balls!" thought everyone. "Little balls of fried dough. Whee."

Little did they know, the real surprise was yet to come.

It was a bitter, sudden, unexpected surprise, like a blast of icy snow in the face.

It was Mistress Death, who sprang into the room and, tearing the skin from her own skull, leapt on Morfeo on this, his happiest night.

Morfeo sat dozing beneath the snowy window unaware that a cursed Fate awaited him. Because Fate doesn't take off weekends or holidays.

A shutter, heavy as a coffin and anchored to the wall for so many years, decided it was tired of life. It detached itself and struck Morfeo squarely in the head. A tremendous blow, a cry that echoed throughout the house, and then nothing.

What do you remember of all of this, Morfeo?

The roof of the ambulance, an EMT laughing and saying "What kind of Christmas party was this? The kid's got a broken skull!" And then the sound of the siren, the yellow light, the bounces and bumps as the ambulance rushed toward a large door that read EMERGENCY ROOM. But it was not Death, not yet. It was a foreign country, a ghost's whisper, a painful astonishment. Morfeo passed out again in a fog of alcohol with blood on his face.

Then, nothing. A brief, endless oblivion.

Morfeo awoke several hours later in a hospital room with twin beds and a view of a wall. Next to him, on the nightstand, a glass of carbonated juice and his toy soldiers. Unfortunately, none of them on a horse.

"What happened?" he asked, his mouth dry. And his tired mother, and his father (who was smoking even though he wasn't supposed to) told him what had happened, and they added "You almost died, you have a bad concussion!" And next to them, sat Death, her mouth full with a hundred half-smoked cigarettes.

After that fateful Christmas night, Morfeo learned many things.

First of all, he learned that there are ceilings. A sky of ceilings, occupying the entire world and hiding the sun, a universe of drawings, stains, stories, and upside down creatures.

Then he learned how many noises people make in their sleep, snoring and speeches and lamentations and groans. He learned that the world is divided between those who sleep well and those who cannot sleep.

His roommate, for example, never slept. At night he would go to the window, and in the morning he'd say "You're lucky, little one, you close your eyes and you sleep. Every night I'm terrified of going to bed." The following year he did fall asleep – forever – from a brain tumor. He had the dark face of a typical fisherman. He used to say, "I became a fisherman for the office hours. You have to get up at four in the morning!"

He hated medicines, but he consumed them like bread. He said that medicines control the world. They heal and they kill, they are bad angels, but more injurious than angelic. Along with oil and weapons, medicines are the ruthlessly beating heart of the economy.

There were eleven bottles on his table, an entire soccer team.

The team had an all-star roster: Riparol, Falqui, Simpatol, Cebion,

D'Aspirini, Rim, Micorenho, Tavori, Legalon, Codeini, Valium.

The coach was a thin and authoritarian IV pole.

The fisherman with the typically dark face had become addicted to tranquilizers and painkillers after his wife's death, and everyone knew it.

And sure enough, on the packaging of the drug sitting on Morfeo's bedside table, in red letters, the manufacturer had carefully not written, "*Danger. Take this for a maximum of three months and then stop.*"

They had not written it in big letters, in huge letters. Three months only, no more. Three months maximum, then go about your business. Tell me straight, warn me, shout it in my face: smoking kills, and this doesn't?

Instead, there was only a very thin, almost translucent, piece of paper. It was folded like a map, called a *bugiardino* – literally, "little liar" in Italian – listing side effects, contraindications, horrible things that happen to one lucky person in ten thousand. It was written in tiny print. In mini-Hittite, in micro-Egyptian, in ancient Asclepian cryptography. Written especially for the elderly, the vision impaired, for those unfamiliar with Greek and Latin.

Morfeo puzzled over that leaflet and read things he would understand only much later: side effects, hypersensitivity to the components, adverse reactions.

It would have been more honest to write: "Once you take this pill, whatever happens is your own goddamn problem." Morfeo, who hadn't met Death yet – but was starting to smell her perfume in drops, pills, and ether – began to wonder, "Who invented this library of elixirs and poisons? Thousands of pages, wouldn't only ten be enough? Did cavemen nod off with the aid of sleeping pills?" Thousands of drugs, diets, panaceas, and IV lines to avoid Death. They want an easy life, those drug merchants. One day, Morfeo would learn of their profits: billions and billions every year, enough to buy and sell whole countries. And out of all that they spent only a tiny fraction on finding better and safer drugs rather than on drugs that are novel just because, and little pills that anesthetize or exhilarate.

In short, they were criminals making the entire suffering world both their market and their guinea pig. The good Morfeo would discover this little by little. Now, from his bed, he was looking at islands and continents and spiders and shadows on the ceiling, with his bandaged head, and blue pajamas, a little crumpled, and the nightly party in his pants.

As companions he had the fisherman's snoring and a small radio, his grandmother's gift, and the Mickey Mouse comic book that smelled of ink and newsstand.

And also a piece of chocolate, and some orange juice for his dry mouth.

He would lie there, waiting for visiting hours to end, with his head bandaged like a soldier, looking at his dozing grandfather, at his mother, who kept shaking her head, at his father smoking and arguing with the nurses.

"Look at my little Spartan, who fights against shutters! My Leonidas!" his grandfather would say, laughing. "A hundred years pass in a flash, and then one day a hundred pounds of wood decide to fall right on your curly little head, Morfeo. Why?"

There was a shadow on the ceiling that looked like an angel. Before falling asleep, Morfeo would look at the angel changing shape and becoming a Native American warrior, then he would feel his eyelids getting heavy, drink the orange juice and silently fart, knowing the dark-faced fisherman would get the blame.

"I have always cheered for the Native Americans," the fisherman would say.

"Christopher Columbus killed two million of them, he has statues everywhere, the heroic discoverer of America. Do you want a statue, Morfeo?. . . Kill someone. Or better yet, kill a lot of someones! If you can't find any Native Americans, find someone else, if you've got a gun and they don't."

A doctor with a very authoritative demeanor entered. He was young but you could already sense that he would get ahead in his career. His name was Dr. Poiana, and he was from a noble medical lineage. He called Morfeo and his parents into his small office. His assistant, a mere child, was a recent graduate named Pietro Ossicino and extremely timid and servile. He handed the x-rays and some papers to his boss.

Dr. Angelo Poiana put his feet on his desk, looked at the x-rays, snorted and said, "The concussion is resolved. The boy can go home."

So young and already so decisive.

Thanks to this oracular pronouncement, Morfeo was discharged after twenty days in the hospital. The fresh air filled his lungs like the best of medicine. The first thing he saw was a blonde girl entering the hospital carrying a bouquet and wearing white shoes with high heels.

She looked like an Angel. The world outside is beautiful. It's nice to remember how it was, thirty years ago.

Morfeo, thirty years later

Morfeo was now thirty-eight years old and, every so often, suffered from depression and knew it. Dr. Poiana was fifty-eight; he was depressed but he didn't know it.

Dr. Poiana, son of Gabriele Poiana, gynecologist, had fortuitously advanced his career by marrying Diana Angela, known as Diangela, daughter of Asmodeo Gheppi, distinguished surgeon. And so he eventually became the respected Professor Angelo Maria Poiana, neurologist, oncologist, and poly-symptomatologist. He had noticed that in those particular fields, the drugs were more numerous and expensive than in others. Immediately on his marriage, he had come into a well-established clinic, courtesy of his father-in-law. Professor Angelo Maria Poiana had a son, Kevin, whom, though he still lived at home, Professor Poiana would not see for weeks at a time. This was a spoiled little Poiana who drank cocktails by the gallon, took loads of pills, and dreamed of becoming a big Poiana dentist, because dentists make good money, and considering that even skeletons have teeth, one might even rake it in post-mortem.

Morfeo had as a companion one Angela Dina, called Angedia. She was a distant cousin of the Poianas, but from the poor branch of the family, defeated in an ancient feud over inheritance. This defeat had made her jealous, restless, and determined to change her hair color at least once a month. She was a colorful, curvy angel who made him suffer and cheated on him. And he suffered because, in his head, he was allowed to cheat but she was not. Sometimes he wanted her, other times he wondered why he wanted someone like her.

Diangela and Angedia looked like sisters. They were both attracted to men they believed to be special, at least at first. Diangela thought Poiana was a great entrepreneur and would accomplish great things in medicine. She had guessed right about the first part. But she had never really loved him. Angela Dina thought Morfeo had the potential to become a world-renowned writer, but she quickly realized that would never make them rich and that she didn't actually like books, preferring fortune tellers and television. Diangela cheated on her husband with discretion, and almost always in highlands, strands, or parklands far away from prying eyes. Angedia, instead, cheated on Morfeo openly, to make him suffer, or perhaps out of an urge to even the score first. Morfeo, on his part, reciprocated. And trying to become someone, he worked nights, he squeezed himself in endless marathons, pressing out his vital juices between sheets of paper, wandered the city, followed a series of upended, impossible schedules. It wasn't long before the darkness of the night invaded his daytime thoughts as well. He became envious of others' success. He became angry and began postulating medical reasons for his failures. One day, after a night of work and cigarettes, everything went black and he had a fainting spell that landed him in the emergency room. It was his mother who convinced him to go see a specialist. He objected, then acquiesced. He felt a great fear inside.

And it was Christmas once again.

His grandparents' house was long gone. Morfeo barely remembered that window underneath the shutter. Thirty years had passed, and now it was a cellular, cybernetic Christmas, no longer as snowy, gray and lifeless as the eyes of a demented old man. Holiday decorations filled the town. Once upon a time, one could stare, enchanted, at a red and gold glass ball. Now one couldn't care less about ten thousand flashing lights.

People still prepared nativity scenes, but now the statuettes were made of plastic unless they were the scattered remains of an antediluvian manger. Nobody made the river out of aluminum foil, any longer. Only the sheep were unchanged, like character actors on the BBC.

Dr. Poiana thought of the upcoming holiday season, unsure, for once, about the diagnosis: would it be more healthful to spend it on an exotic island or at an exclusive ski resort?

He had his feet up, in the same way and on the same desk as thirty years before. Time had stopped. Pietro Ossicino, still his mild, serious, servile assistant, stood by his side next to a skeleton on a stand, playing with the bones and making them clack. Professor Poiana looked at the same avenue of lime trees he had seen again and again – and hated again and again – for thirty years. "I will finally escape," he thought, "I will finally escape this run-down Hell of hospital pavilions, broken toilets, and vomit, from the screams and beatings, from these drugs on which I earn twenty percent. And this will all be nothing but bulldozers, dust and debris, a beautiful demolition. And then, out of the weeds, an apartment building will rise. All this pain will be buried and forgotten. I will have a modern clinic and dedicate myself to my true calling, the depression of the wealthy and the study of why-those-who-have-everything-have-nothing."

On the oak desk he had inherited from his father, the gynecologist, the Big Poiana, sat an ashtray filled with reeking cigarette butts, a bronze Mercury, a picture of Diana Angela with pale purple hair, her son and lover in the background, and a stack of medical journals. In a closet as big as a library, were the great books of medical knowledge, the medical uncertain-knowledge, and even the medical non-knowledge. There were hundreds of samples of drugs of all kinds, drugs to make you stoned, drugs to cheer you up, drugs to numb your pain. And eye drops. Old and new names, and old drugs recycled as brand new. And three x-ray plates, large, black, transparent. Morfeo's skull. Then laboratory reports, data and charts. Blood cells, erythrocytes, blood turned into fuel.

Poiana now sighed, thereby creating a certain suspense. He was preparing to give his opinion.

Morfeo stared at the floor while his white-haired mother held his hand. They did not look at each other.

"I have dedicated myself to this case while ignoring others far more serious," said Poiana, "because of our distant kinship." He made a broad gesture as if to indicate the distance. "And today, I wish I had some different news for you, my dear lady, I wish I could tell you I have doubts," (his assistant, Pietro Ossicino, winced behind him) ". . . but I am afraid there is no doubt. Your son. . .

is epileptic. Tests confirm it and it explains his anger, his depression, his. . . minor, yet serious acts of irrationality that have brought him to the attention of the authorities even as a child."

"But that happened only once. . ."

"I'm a doctor, I'm not interested in politics, but I understand what you're saying. I was a hothead once myself. But politics isn't real life. In politics, everyone is entitled to their opinion. But in real life, someone has to make a decision. Medicine isn't democratic. We don't get to vote on a diagnosis. What we've done," he said with a certain professional pride, "is conduct a top-notch consultation. We showed the test results to the finest specialists. To my brother and to the greatest European expert, Malak, from Berlin, who happens to be a friend of mine. And so, I repeat the word: e-pi-lep-sy.

Your son will have an almost normal life but he must be kept under control. Regular hours, no debauchery at night. No work for three months. But above all, lots and lots of drugs. Here's the prescription."

And he took out a giant sheet of paper that looked like a medieval edict.

"Remember: he has to take them every day, without fail. It is your responsibility, as well as mine."

"No. . . no doubts at all?" asked Morfeo's mother in a whisper.

"Madam," said Pietro Ossicino, the assistant, "in these cases there is always room for doubt but. . ."

"But as I said, experience and expertise decide." Poiana interrupted authoritatively. "Pietro, go get the bottles of phenobarbital, valproate and all the rest. The therapy begins today."

Morfeo's mother began sobbing, her tears dripping on the floor.

"Doctor, how can I tell his father? He has just been fired. And Morfeo's work. . ."

"That's not a medical problem," Poiana said, now really annoyed. "Dr. Ossicino, stop playing with the skeleton, open the medicine cabinet and prepare the patient's first treatment. And don't screw it up. . . again!"

"Yes, sir," said the assistant, "but I thought, perhaps. . . I could go with this lady to break the news to her husband."

"Sure. Why not? Let's all go! The patients can treat themselves while we're out." sneered Poiana.

"Madam," Dr. Ossicino said quietly, "epilepsy can be cured nowadays, it's a dangerous condition, but we can keep it under control. However, beware of him not taking his drugs. One day, Morfeo could have a major seizure and. . . goodbye! Or he might be driving his car, lose consciousness and go off the road. . ."

"He only owns a scooter," Morfeo's mother said.

"On the other hand," Pietro Ossicino mused, "he's never actually had a real convulsion. And, you know, after suffering that concussion as a child. . . that massive shutter crashing into his head. . . according to his chart. . ."

"I read it closely myself, let's get it over with!" Poiana said, slapping the desk. "We are not here to relive the last century of the patient's medical history. Does a shutter on your head thirty years ago count more than the opinion of thirty specialists today?"

"Well, sometimes, the stress associated with an old accident. . ." Ossicino began.

Dr. Poiana angrily snapped the folder with the x-rays shut and stalked out of the room, calling over his shoulder, "Dr. Ossicino, quit wittering and stop getting these people's hopes up, or you can stay here and rot when I move to the new clinic. I believe in medicines, you believe in happy talk. You just try and cure a cancer patient with a lullaby. If you're this indecisive and weak, you'll never amount to anything as a doctor."

It was in that moment, as the final verdict was pronounced, that a swish of wings could be heard, and through the window could be seen, in the avenue with the lime trees, the Bad Angel leaving the hospital, escorted by two orderlies, each carrying a cardboard box. The Bad Angel was wearing an old prison shirt, and had dirty, long hair hanging past his shoulders. He wasn't exactly a man, nor exactly a woman, and neither an angel nor a demon. He was Gadariel, with broken, frayed wings, shattered by years of sorrow. The great warrior Gadariel, Gaddo to his friends.

He was leaving the hospital for some cheerful concentration camp somewhere in the neighborhood. As he disappeared from view, he turned his head and looked at Morfeo as if to say: "We shall meet again."

The Angel's Freedom

Gadariel looked at the drawings he had painted with the feathers of his wings on the bark of the lime trees over all the long years of his captivity. All his dreams. The orderlies could never look him in the eye. They were afraid. The wind of his wings was pain, his look unbearable. What kind of madness was his? Angelic one day, violent the next. And those endless monologues! "Gentlemen, I rebelled against God because he could have done more. I have sworn allegiance to man, not God. My pity is forged here on earth, not from the lofty detachment of heaven. God is only that which is done in the name of God."

But that was all over now.

He was leaving.

"They are carrying off my life in two cardboard boxes," he was thinking. "They are carrying off my books, my handful of clothes, my notebooks written in angelic language, my blood stains. My drugs, my drawings, the letters that I wrote to myself.

"My chipped drinking glass, my dull knife.

"They can't carry off the air in which I flew.

"My bed, gone, with its nightmares, its raging curses, its tears, leavened only by fleeting dreams.

"By this time tomorrow, the walls of this asylum will be rubble. They have unscrewed the taps, carried off the stretchers, the restraint beds, the ties and the ropes. A new building, seven stories of life, will be born here, rising to the sky.

"Those who carry off my life are insensitive to the pain connected to these things. They are men with gloomy faces, alien and unknown. Or, perhaps, they hear a distant, incomprehensible echo of my lament and they are eager to hustle me to the gate and send me on my way. I sense that they suffer as I do.

I would like to lay my wings on their shoulders. But they are afraid.

"They have closed the garden gate. The barren lime trees, where I spent so many hours wandering, will die. The sparrows, all those generations of winged friends who fluttered around me, will be gone. The cat ran off a week ago.

"The dry, crumbling ivy barely remembers me banging my head against the wall in my night rages.

"This place of agony, and cells, and night screams will become something else. But the building that takes its place will house my ghost forever, and the souls, shining with fever, of all those who died here.

"Here we danced, chained, and laughed, toothless.

"They are taking away the crucifixes, the paintings, the lamps and the chairs, even the one used by a friend of mine to hang himself.

"What will remain as a witness to all my years in this place?

"Only the sky through the branches will remain, and now I'm falling into it.

"Somewhere, there are places where you can pretend to not feel pain, where, for just a moment, everything seems suspended, interrupted, magical. Places where people can breathe.

"You are only happy when you are cheating Death.

"Even only one minute, one hour, one morning will be enough, at least for me.

"But I will never truly forget this loneliness. You can never forget true loneliness.

"Now the Bad Angel, Gadariel, has a job, three things to do, as it is written in the one true gospel, the one recounting the war of the rebellious Angels, the Book of the Broken Wings.

"First, I must help Morfeo. Morfeo doesn't know it yet, but he's expecting a child. I suppose I'll have to help them both.

"Then I'll have to help his father, old Giobbe.

"And finally, I must do something to snuff out a tiny bit of the world's pain. In our existence, there is just a drop more Good than Evil, a tiny drop. We must all gather that drop every day.

"When I'm finished, I'll finally have my new wings, noble and shining in the light.

"Certainly, no demon can stop me, because I am also a demon, my wings turn black at night. I am a rebel. I have set my face against the Master of Healing, the God of Death.

"My wounds still bleed, but you can no longer see them.

"No, I won't always be good, that's not my way. Is it anyone's? But it will be nice to live among people, with open wings protecting them from too much pain. Morfeo, take shelter in the shadow of my plumage. I'll give you a Native American warrior, one that Columbus never found, who lived a long and happy life with his tribe, hidden away in an enchanted valley.

"Open the way, Guardians, I am in haste. I must save a man from the flames of Hell, though they are of his own making. It is we who bring the flames of Hell to Earth. In the beginning they are no more than a match, a tiny flame, but soon everything burns, and it's too late. But perhaps I am still in time.

"Believe in me. I'm your Bad Angel."

The End of Giobbe

Six-thirty in the morning. Fog, headlights, damp, gloom. Giobbe, Morfeo's father, had been pedaling for an hour. He had crossed the entire city, contemplating the houses as they lit up and the people as they left their homes. He had heard curses, seen fatigue, smelled coffee. In the air hung the universal desire to remain in bed, the wife's hair on the pillow, the husband's broken snoring. He remembered what he said every morning, half asleep, the same thing that Morfeo would repeat an hour later: a vow of revenge. "Someday, someone will pay for this."

Hours of lost sleep just to attend a pointless lesson, to tighten one more bolt, to make a billionaire industrialist a little bit richer, to cover six freezing miles on a scooter or a bicycle.

Morfeo got up early these days. He wrote articles for a foreign newspaper. He had taken the anti-epileptic cocktail of drugs for a few months, but they made him so numb he couldn't work. Then came the news that Angedia was expecting a child. This caught Morfeo by surprise and he didn't know what to think. He was frightened, but also somehow hopeful. So he swore off the anti-epileptic drugs, turning instead to more sedate sedatives. He didn't know they had the same powers of binding and diminishing. Perhaps he took them because it was the easiest way for him to deal with such complex situations. Dr. Poiana had probably already forgotten the man he had terrorized with his hasty diagnosis. But its effects were all too real and, for Morfeo and his family, the traces of the Angels slipped through their fingers and vanished on that day.

Anyway, this foggy morning saw the end of Giobbe's story.

The city was searching through the smog for a glimmer of light; trams rattled and a dog followed along behind Giobbe's bike, with that typical, unaware-of-death happiness that animals share. It was a hairy old mutt, trotting proudly, like a horse escorting a President to an inauguration, closely monitoring the asphalt and sniffing at piss spots with a gourmet air. *You're in quite a hurry there, aren't you, Mr. Cyclist? Beautiful weather we're having. The fog is lovely.* There were so many bikes carrying anger, dreams, and shivering men just like Giobbe, the army of labor, and each man measured the miserable portion of life ahead of him by the rhythm of his pedaling.

And of all that army, the one with the smallest portion was Giobbe the Humiliated. He had only a shred left, less than an hour.

He carried a gasoline can hanging from the handlebars, clanging like a bell as it swung back and forth in the silence of the dawn. The can held only a few liters of gas. He had no money for more than that. His legs burned as he pedaled up the hill and toward the drive that led to the big factory.

Struggling until the very end, always struggling.

Giobbe could finally see the flat, gray shape of the factory where he had worked for so many years. The smokestacks and the roofs receded into the fog, an alpine range he had climbed so many times to repair the veins and the arteries and the electric wires.

Fog was his constant companion. At times, it even seemed to bar his way as if to say, "Think again, Giobbe.

"Here on earth, you think me gray and sad, but in the heavens, I am the clouds that Angels, rebellious and free, brush at dawn, like sheep's wool, or a woman's hair.

"And these Angels say, 'We must go down into the world. Mankind needs us. And as a gift we shall bring a reliquary containing an extra hour of sleep.'"

Giobbe stopped pedaling and lit his last cigarette; he tasted it, a strawberry at the edge of the abyss, a lark flying over the firing squad. He didn't think of *ifs* or *buts* or *how* it could have gone differently. He saw the faces of his loved ones, but he was already far away. He only wept for a moment, a brief sob, echoed by the dog's whining.

He thought angrily of the pink slip in his pocket, and along with the cigarette smoke, he blew out a curse. The pink slip informing him he had been fired, a month ago, now rustling in his pocket, along with a goodbye note written and rewritten so many times.

He considered those two pieces of paper, so different, and yet between them, they contained the story of his life: the final chapter written by Fate and the choices of others, the epilogue, his last, painful, freedom.

Every suicide is unique. Don't judge them. Feel pity, great pity, for them. And in some cases, honor their courage. And give tombstones to each of them, and a photo on a bedside table. Photos last longer than we do. It is odd that we call them snapshots.

So he sat on the bench in front of that pale caterpillar, the enormous factory that devoured curses and bolts.

How many times before had he been in that place, at that hour, talking with his colleagues, a strange mixture of conversations: sad, angry, happy, playful? There were cigarette butts everywhere.

Now he was truly alone. His canine acquaintance had found another bicycle to follow.

He had to wait, however. He needed a witness, at least one.

He saw a car slowly advancing on the road, and also a three-wheeled truck driven by a big guy, an *extracomunitario,* with a load of bags and suitcases, a self-made titan of industry.

"It's showtime," he thought, "let's try and not screw up, for once."

First, he poured gasoline on one arm, then on the other and, finally, onto his chest.

But there wasn't all that much to go around and he soon ran out.

"Oh crap, what if it isn't enough?" he thought. "But no, it will be. It must." So he shook the last drop onto his head, spitting and sneezing. He had been breathing poison all his life. This was the last time.

He pulled out his lighter and took a last look at his surroundings.

He saw the car still advancing slowly, a flock of chiseling seagulls flying off towards the incinerator. He could also see a plane in the sky. But the man in the three-wheeled truck had stopped because his load was collapsing. Giobbe wanted to cry.

"Goddamit! Not now!"

He flicked the lighter and felt a thousand teeth run up his arm.

"Let it be quick," he thought.

It was actually quite quick; something like an enormous wing blocked the sky, covered him, extinguished the flames.

He found himself on the ground. His hands hurt badly and his first impression was the stench of burnt flesh.

But he was alive, there on the ground. And hovering over him he could see the face – a face he had not seen for thirty years – of his old friend Gaddo, the Bad Angel. Gaddo was laughing at him and carrying an ancient coat, still smoking, in his hands.

The apparition spoke. "You're not even good at killing yourself."

"Gaddo. . . how . . . how did you know I was here?"

"I saw you as I was flying by," Gadariel said, "or maybe your wife told me you were out with a can of gasoline attached to your bike. So here I am. And just in time, it seems."

"Gaddo! . . . But I thought they had you locked up!"

"They let me go, too expensive for the government to keep, I guess. Crazy people cost much less when they're free. But tell me, how is Morfeo doing? You two were my only visitors back then."

"He's doing well enough. He had been taking anti-epilepsy drugs, but now he's off them and taking other crap instead. He lives for his son. He writes for a newspaper at the moment, but they are laying everyone off. But enough about us. Where the hell have you been all this time?"

"Oh, the usual. Prisons, asylums, I flew, I fought, I got beaten up, but I've never forgotten my friends. Come on, I'll take you to the emergency room, you smell like a burnt roast. Even ceasing to exist is beyond your capabilities. You merit neither Heaven nor Hell. Let's go, my cooked goose."

"And how do we get there?"

"Hey, you! Yes, you on the three-wheeled truck!" Gadariel shouted, "Give us a ride to the hospital and we'll buy something from you."

Giobbe was holding his roasted hand; the *extracomunitario* looked at them, unflappable, like he had seen this sort of thing before and had become a bit blasé about it. Gadariel continued teasing

Giobbe unmercifully, even after they had arrived at the emergency room and had an audience of variously damaged bystanders.

"You're a terrible cook, you useless, suicidal man. Hey! What are you looking at? No, he didn't injure himself making pizza. He got fired. Yes, fired, damn it, don't you know what that means?"

He argued with the orderly wheeling Giobbe inside on a stretcher and almost beat him up. He consoled a mother who had brought in a little boy with a high fever. Even in the emergency room of a hospital, thirty years later, he was still himself, the Bad Angel.

The Dinner

A peaceful evening, a few years later.

Here they all were, our happy once-upon-a-time-young people, not yet decrepit, celebrating Morfeo's birthday.

Morfeo looked greyer and sported the melancholy jollity of the celebrated.

Angedia, his wife, was there, too, even though they were now living apart. She currently had dull brown hair that would have looked sad on a mouse. She was pale, but not resigned, and still in the hunt for that special man who would give her everything she didn't deserve.

Their son, the Little Prince, somewhat bored because the adults tended to listen to each other more than him even though, at five, he was certainly wiser than any of them.

His mini-girlfriend Giuly, with a beautiful, sunny smile.

Giuly's father, Orio, a silent and bearded psychiatrist, who spoke little and missed less.

Pompeo, former program director of KBGZ, The Rabbit 101, an independent radio station that used to broadcast endless hours of drug-fueled poetry and encouraged everyone to resist, trust the bunny, and believe that the Government, riven by the internal contradictions of capitalism, would soon collapse. Instead, it was The Rabbit 101, riven by the internal contradictions of trying to turn a profit, that collapsed (and was snapped up by a successful country-western chain of radio stations) as did Pompeo himself who died of an overdose, after writing a six-thousand-page, single-spaced manuscript that has now disappeared.

Picozza, former worker, always active and with magic hands, who kept saying, "Comrades, here there's little to talk about and a lot to do." And he was one of the few who did.

Big Vincenzo, who spoke only of soccer and politics, and kept repeating, in a baritone voice, that one only had to find the right tactics either to score goals or to win elections. He also laughed a lot and ate like a horse.

Carlini, the school teacher, who understood everything but explained nothing while surveying the world with pity in his eyes.

Sandro, gentle, fragile, a music lover, who would end up like Jeff Buckley, dead in a river.

Giobbe was not there. He hadn't left his house in quite a long time, embarrassed by his red, scarred hands that resembled a *zampone* and reminded him of that ridiculous, terrible, horrible, no good, very bad day. Neither was Morfeo's mother.

A blonde, teen-aged girl also sat at the table. She never said a word but somehow drew everyone's eye, even the women's.

"Who are you?" Sandro asked.

"I'm Eleonora, but everyone calls me Elpis, and I'm the Sister. . ."

"Whose sister?"

"Diangela's, Angedia's, everyone's sister. . ." laughed the girl.

"Are you some kind of step-sister? Adopted?"

"Why does it matter? Don't you want me here?"

"No, no, I'm not saying that," Sandro said, "but. . ."

"Then shut up and eat. . ." the girl snapped.

"Well, well!" Carlini snorted, "So many mysteries. . ."

"You leave her alone!" said the Little Prince.

And that was that. But Morfeo somehow knew that the smiling young girl would come back into his life.

At the center of the table, Gadariel, the Bad Angel, dominated the scene. Recently discharged from yet another halfway house, he had returned to remind everyone that, after thirty years, nothing had changed. The injustices were still the same, and so were the masters and the drugs. He provoked the entire company ranting, "We're all intoxicated, drugged, chained. We're still in the old hospital wing, full of screaming and beating. They've built seven floors over that wing. Perhaps now there will be a few more immigrants. But the pain is still there. And at night, from underground, the cries of the inmates still shake the walls.

Uncontrollable, fat, dirty, his anger still pristine, he shouted, "How's it going, Morfeo? Are we still making a revolution?"

Morfeo was over forty, he had separated from Angedia, but in the meantime a miracle had been born, his all-consuming love for his son, the Little Prince, who lived with him and was his joy, the gift that redeemed all pain, and that he loved with an anxious and protective love, but a true one, nonetheless.

Only for him was he capable of sacrifice, only for him would his selfishness shatter. He had managed to publish two books. He wrote for newspapers. He played his part in the games of petty jealousies and the rituals of literature.

And he had forgotten the word 'epileptic'. But he always worked at night. There were hours of lonely writing, alcoholic friends, dinners at four in the morning. And it was catching up with him. He was strung out almost all the time and rarely slept.

One night he collapsed in the middle of the street and landed in the emergency room again.

"Convulsion triggered by nervous exhaustion." said the report, *"Neurological follow-up recommended."* And just like that, the old word, epilepsy, was tip-toeing back on stage like not a day had gone by. He tried getting an appointment with Dr. Poiana, but it was impossible. So he wrote to him and, through Diangela, managed to have his letter delivered.

He received a terse note in response: "I confirm my original diagnosis. I also confirm that you are a fool who refused to follow the recommended treatment. This episode was not triggered by nervous exhaustion. It's much worse.

It's your congenital epilepsy. I thought so then, and this proves I was right. Control your condition with appropriate drugs, and if you have any further questions, you needn't consult me. Consult Dr. Ossicino instead."

Oh yes, the shy Pietro Ossicino.

He had served Poiana with hatred and devotion and, at the moment, was suffering through a career crisis. Having just been screwed out of a promotion to Department Head, his mind wasn't really on his work. Thus, when asked by *his* assistant about Morfeo's case, he hedged like a sort of wishy-washy Poiana. "Anti-epileptics! Tell whoever it is to give benzodiazepines a try instead. They're the best selling drugs in Italy, so they must be good! Half of Italy's finest citizens take this stuff and don't even know what it is."

They came in a white, reassuring box, and they actually did work, at least at the beginning. And on the box, in large red letters, the manufacturer had carefully not written,

"Danger. Take this for a maximum of three months and then stop."

There were only a few cryptic hints about dependency, written in mini-hieroglyphs, on the leaflet. So Morfeo reached what we might call an 'equilibrium', that is, he became intoxicated and dependent without knowing it. He lived with the little pillbox always in his pocket. He thought that chemistry was his friend, and didn't sense the danger. Like the old memory of Death. Do you remember, Morfeo, when you were sitting under the shutter and the world was only life?

"A toast! A toast to those of us who can't face reality and meet it head on nonetheless," Gadariel said. "I'll see you at our next collective dinner, maybe twenty years from now. We'll all be aged, or perhaps gone. We'll get drunk and brawl over politics. We'll become martyrs or murderers. We'll be vintage goods displayed in flea-market stalls, like old sweaters and military boots. We'll be old yellow leaves in a scrapbook, and a girl's signature, 'Joyce Allison, 1894,' on the flyleaf of a book by Lewis Carroll that I sold yesterday. We'll be little lead soldiers, and some of us will be dead, except me, because I I'm an Angel.

Part Two

Many years later

Gadariel, the Bad Angel, disappeared, blown away with the clouds. He spent time in Brazil and dealt cocaine. There was a rumor that he had died. He fought with some revolutionaries. Got shot. Lost an eye. Along the way he ended up back in a mental hospital. He might have also gotten married three times, though he couldn't really say. His memory wasn't what it used to be.

Giobbe died of cancer after smoking sixteen million cheap cigarettes.

In the coffin, he resembled an extraterrestrial, with his yellow fingers and skeletal frame.

Angedia first ended up in a cult and then, half-insane, locked in her house. Old age came to her suddenly and pinned her in front of her TV.

Diangela eventually used her residual beauty to seduce Professor Gufi, a colleague of Professor Poiana. She gave blow jobs to entire hospital wings and oncology conferences and her husband's chain of medical clinics greatly benefited from it. Then, one day, her beauty was gone and only silicone, anger, and bitchy friends remained along with a hundred and thirty-six bracelets in a jewelry box, that someone (she thought a Romanian) had stolen from her.

The Little Prince became a talented musician, and although he had a colorful personality, he somehow managed well enough.

Morfeo spent the best years of his life with him. Then things started to change.

He and the Little Prince began to live apart. The boy-that-was was becoming a man.

And Morfeo continued gobbling those soothing benzodiazepine candies like a gluttonous child.

Life went on, and they all were taking different paths.

Giulia, the Little Prince's girlfriend, married an Australian and went on to sell Italian ice cream with flavors like Bananapolis and Nappuccino in Moololaba, on the Gold Coast.

Pompeo's book was found in a dresser. Nobody read more than ten pages, although it was a compelling narrative of his times.

Piccozza made beautiful foam toys for disabled children, organized village fairs, and built giant figures for political demonstrations. He had magical, wrinkled hands as elegant and beautiful as tree branches. He remained generous, and enjoyed entertaining children. He never gave up. He kept watch over the brook in his village, to make sure no one caught the last whitefish.

Big Vincenzo ate thirty tons of pigs, had three heart attacks, and continued to play soccer until the thirtieth minute of the semifinal of the national tournament of veteran's clubs. They were losing one to two when he collapsed.

His last words were, "Oh, shit! We could have gotten at least a draw!"

Carlini kept saying that he understood. Eventually, he turned that into a career.

Sandro ended up as a bouquet of flowers on a bridge.

And one day, shortly before a Christmas very different from its predecessors, Morfeo was walking down a snowy street. He was looking for a present for his son when what to his wondering eyes should appear but a gray, familiar face that was drinking a beer.

The gray face returned his gaze and stood up.

"It's Morfeo, isn't it?"

"Yes. And I remember you," said Morfeo. "You're Dr. Ossicino, Professor Poiana's assistant."

"I remember your case. You're the boy we treated many years ago for a concussion after a freak accident. . . and then you went back to Dr. Poiana for a consultation. . . I've often thought about your case. I was never comfortable with it. . . Tell me, have you had any seizures over the last few years?"

"Never. Oh, I've had plenty of other problems, fits of anger and anxiety, but never seizures or convulsions. . ."

"I knew it!" Pietro said, pounding his hand on the table. "That Poiana is a pompous ass. He always took the easy way out. Do you know what kind of career he had? He has three luxury clinics, Villa Santa Grazia, Villa Santa Giuliana, and Villa Santa Gemma." Pietro smiled ruefully. "But he's dying of

49

cancer, and his patron saints can't intercede for him. He has three cars and two yachts and he's going nowhere, except to hell. He has who knows how many houses and hundreds of beds, but he can't sleep at night. He worked very little, smoked and drank quite a lot, spent his time with prostitutes, lied whenever it suited him, and accepted money from anyone. He's a consultant for nine pharmaceutical companies. But he's also a skeleton in a bed. You know, I pity him, I really do. But I pity many others a lot more."

"I'm sorry," said Morfeo.

"I'm sorry I didn't have the courage to speak up back then. . ." Pietro Ossicino sighed. "The examinations, the x-rays, were all sloppily done. A radiologist friend of his did them between tennis matches. I really should have insisted that your case needed further investigation, and I've always felt guilty about that, but he was addicted to drugs, or at least to selling them. I suppose I was, too, at least a little. He taught me to keep patients subdued, controlled by chemicals and our god-like powers. He taught me to always do the easy thing and never assume any responsibility. And I was even worse than he was. I did have doubts and I chose a glorious career by his side anyway. But he's dying now and I've finally clawed back a little bit of my soul." He took a deep breath and stood up a little straighter as if suddenly free of a heavy weight, "We have the chance to correct the mistakes we made so long ago. Morfeo, please, agree to another examination."

"More tests? No, please. . ."

"Listen carefully. There is something new, something that can finally get to the bottom of your problem. Come to my office, the day after tomorrow. You need to know about CEDS."

"What's that?"

"A new tool for diagnosing cases of epilepsy. It's already widely used in Canada, but pharmaceutical companies are trying to keep it out of Europe. I managed to get one for testing and you can be a test. Come and see me on Thursday. I'll book you an appointment for four o'clock."

Another test. More white corridors and the smell of ether. More endless waiting.

In hearing those two words, Morfeo re-lived an entire lifetime of anxiety in a single, shuddering breath. The sounds of the ambulance, an entire world in the ceiling of a hospital room, his head throbbing, the first silent hiss of Death, his failures, the love thrown away, his dead friends, his lost illusions, all the betrayals, and all the things he had never done. And, worst of all, the separation from his Little Prince and the end of all those wonderful years. His equilibrium was shattered. If there was a way back to the light, it led through darkness. Fate was leading him down a road that would either leave him wandering lost or lead him to discover, once again, the traces of the Angels.

After all, it was just another test. Perhaps it would be fine. The only joy is cheating Death. Only after sickness can there be healing. And after Death, something better than Death, a purer, softer air. We don't have the words for it, not the believers, not the blasphemers, not the killers or the victims, not the Poianas, not the doctors working for free in Africa, not the Native Americans, not even Christopher

52

Columbus. All the world's languages can only hint at it, but that hint is the trace of the Angels.

The Magic Machine

So one sunny afternoon Morfeo showed up at Villa Santa Gemma, Poiana's newest luxury clinic. It was surrounded by a green park full of flowers and shrubs, lots of cars you'd find at country clubs, and had three full floors of nurses in scrubs. Pietro Ossicino had finally become a Department Head. Long corridors, red armchairs, seats overflowing with battalions of patients, the anger of those who waited, the arrogance of those who knew Somebody – or even the right orderly – and didn't wait. There were people who cleaned everywhere, pouring bleach on the floor and spritzing odorous disinfectant on everything. There were people to dust the ficuses. The place rang with bells and buzzers and with the creaking of litters carrying people whose faces were either utterly serene or utterly mad from the after-effects of anesthesia. Teams of busy, jolly, sweaty, and, occasionally, angry doctors bustled in and out of operating rooms. In this place, lives were being saved, and that was important. In this place, the miracle of healing and the great scam of pacifying pills went hand in hand. As in Poiana's old office, there was an entire army made up of drops, little boxes, tablets, capsules, and bottles, all locked inside a large white closet and under the command of the great General Pietro Ossicino.

On his desk was a photo of his wife and one of his son, an action figure of Cyrano de Bergerac, and many, many medical journals, twice, three times more than in the old days when he was a mere assistant. And hanging on the wall, swinging gently, a skeleton, perhaps the same one that was in Poiana's office so many years ago. Skeletons never grow old. They never change, their skulls grin endlessly, effortlessly, throwing in our faces their eternal youth.

Morfeo and Pietro didn't stop in Pietro's office. Instead, they journeyed through long, empty corridors, like those of an airport.

"Come along, come along," said Pietro breathlessly, "It's just down here. It's truly amazing, what I'm going to show you, the first in Italy!"

Morfeo stood in front of a large, blue door of frosted glass featuring a seal inscribed with an angel holding a human brain in his hands as if it were Yorick's skull. Over the door was a sign that said "Authorized Personnel Only," and an inscription that to Morfeo, in his terror, seemed to say:

Through me you pass into the city of fear
Through me you pass into eternal pain
You question our most high decrees in vain
Abandon hope all ye who enter here.

But what it actually said was,

CEDS
Computerized Epilepsy Diagnostic System

It was like stepping onto the bridge of the Discovery One spacecraft, in the movie *2001: A Space Odyssey*, a white kingdom of monitors, pulsing lines and control consoles. Our spaceship was hurtling toward a vast, microscopic universe of new scientific findings and diagnoses. But the way was dangerous and our intrepid explorers were constantly under attack by pill-shooting pharmaceutical Death Stars. New information meant new doubts, which was bad, and spending more money on research, which was worse. Everybody dies eventually, regardless.

There was a buzzing noise and a bluish glow suffused the room. Captain Pietro Ossicino called over his assistant, a blonde with glasses and a white lab coat, and said, "Doctor, prepare the patient."

The Patient (who had once been Morfeo) was prepared, caged in a translucent vertical pipe that could have been a time machine in yet another movie, greased with creams and darted with electrodes like a Saint Sebastian.

It was then that he realized that, in a corner, sat a mysterious man with a flowing white beard; a Greek divinity or an alien visitor from another dimension.

"May I introduce Dr. Malak, the world's leading expert in epilepsy and seizure conditions? Don't move," said Ossicino, while flashes of lasers and a buzz of celestial spheres filled the room, "the test has begun. Please remain perfectly still."

Morfeo closed his eyes.

"Aha. . ." whispered Pietro Ossicino the first time, in an exploratory tone.

"Aha. . ." he said a second time, doubtful. Dr. Malak remained impassive.

"Aha," he repeated the third time, happy. Dr. Malak raised an eyebrow.

"Aha!" he shouted triumphantly. Dr. Malak stood up and walked over to the monitor, observing it millimeter by millimeter, pixel by pixel.

Then the God spoke, in his alien tongue.

"You zee that zcreen there in the middle, Mizter Morfeo? Well, here iz the example of the brain of ein epileptic. It'z all *rote*, red-orange colored, inflamed, a hellish *teufel*, a demon. And then here iz the image from your examination. A zmall red-orange zpot, like a brush-stroke made by Van Gogh. The zign left by that colozzal blow—the shutter falling on your head, from fifty years ago. Doctor Ozzicino told me about it. It'z damage from your concuzzion, worzened by age. You're not epileptic, you've never been, never, *jamais, niemals*."

And then the God disappeared. He was a good doctor. He had always worked twenty hours a day and had pursued his profession as a soldier honors his duty, to the last of his strength and the end of his life. And even now he was there, at his station, ready for battle.

Morfeo said nothing while Ossicino's assistant scrubbed him clean of sauces and creams.

But in his silence, a thousand thoughts crowded his head.
And one in particular.

"You . . . you drugged me, poisoned me, for years and years with dangerous, pointless chemicals, with drugs I didn't need!"

"Well, that was really mostly Professor Poiana," said Pietro, his eyes lowered.

"But you, too. You allowed it. . ."

"You allowed it, too. You weren't obliged to take those drugs, you must have felt you were getting some benefit from them. You agreed to that 'equilibrium'. As for me, I admit my mistake, I was young, in awe of Poiana's experience. . . I didn't dare voice my doubts and concerns. But that was then. Now everything can be fixed."

"Fixed? How?"

"Just stop taking the drugs you've been prescribed. We'll detox you. It will take six months, at most a year, and then you'll be free. I'll give you the name of a specialist. And cheer up! Now we're sure that you're not epileptic. Would you prefer if you were and had to keep taking the drugs? Doesn't this finally give you some peace?"

And Morfeo realized there was no escape, only new pain that he must endure. If he wanted to cheat Death yet again, enduring the pain would be the price of his new life. Little did he know what that bargain would cost him.

The Road to Hell

It is fair to ask why it never occurred to Morfeo to detox himself until Dr. Ossicino suggested it. But he had never fully considered his situation before and he didn't now, rushing into battle without knowing his enemy.

He thought he could do it on his own, that it would be easy, drop by drop, day by day. After all, half of the world was immersed in a haze of sleeping capsules, pain pills, and mood-altering tablets. Surely a method had been worked out to stop taking them. But there was no method; the pharmaceutical companies had never really bothered to study that. And why should they? Getting people to stop gobbling their candy wasn't their business model. The weapons dealers of the world are only concerned with getting the bullets in. Getting them out is someone else's problem.

Of course, Morfeo obsessively consulted the Internet and lost himself in a maelstrom of terminology and half-understood medical studies: Lorazepam, Diazepam, Bentazepam, dosage tables, the Ashton protocols. He'd just cut back by a milligram a day and he'd be fine, right? Surely everything he had read must apply to his specific case! We're all the same; lab rats in a maze.

He took the road from which there is no return and no way forward; a maze without maps. A road that can change your life, but you won't know how until there is no turning back. Morfeo knew this would be difficult, but he was convinced he could make his way alone. You begin at the beginning, he thought, and eventually you reach the end. How hard could it really be?

It wasn't a simple matter of dosages, however. People are funny things and there is no chart with the exact dosage for bringing peace or warding off insanity. There were many things he had not understood about himself.

He would come to realize later that he had placed his faith in drugs the way some people place their faith in a televangelist. The equilibrium he thought he had achieved was false. The wonders of chemistry and the seduction of a world of herbs and valerian, decoctions and miraculous remedies that he thought he had harnessed were as powerful as the industry that supplied them was criminal.

On the Internet alone, he found thirteen million ways to beat anxiety, insomnia, and depression, each provided with its own method of payment, Visa, MasterCard or American Express. Some even took Paypal. Thirteen million falsehoods and frauds sprinkled with perhaps a thousand truths that had actually been studied or carefully analyzed.

In the fog of his addiction, in the anger of his anxiety, Morfeo did not realize that his love for his son had come to a wonderful but terrible dénouement. That addiction was even stronger than the chemical one, and fighting one addiction with a stronger one did not appear, not even once, in all his Internet researches.

But even this addiction had its share of pain. Morfeo would suffer a thousand torments simply by not hearing his voice on the phone for a few hours. His concern and anxiety for the angry, musical Little Prince had become all-consuming.

He waited anxiously for each appointment, and only when his son's face appeared in the distance could he finally relax. He took to calling the Little Prince's friends and inventing excuses to find out where he was. He suffered all the torments of waiting and separation. He yearned to shield his son from every pain, every sorrow. Even his son's gestures of affection were to him sweet and terrible at the same time. Morfeo believed he could only truly love his own flesh and blood and his love was total, attentive, daily, present, crazy.

It's hard to say why Morfeo had chosen to raise his child by himself and why he often resisted sharing his son's life even with his mother, Angedia. He sometimes hated her and more seldom, when he sensed she shared his responsibility for their child, loved her. He often thought of Elpis, the mysterious step-sister, without knowing why. He had seen her only twice, but he had been struck by her, he had sensed the snow-white flutter of a wing. He only knew that she had lived in Scandinavia and had two children. He liked the way she spoke of them. Diangela had children and didn't want them. Angedia had one but didn't notice.

For the first time in his life, Morfeo thought that he, too, wanted to be part of a proper family. Morfeo used to laugh at happy loving couples and only collected affairs. Pleasant, erotic affairs, that would, inevitably, be brought to nothing by the simple passage of time. But it was enough. Morfeo was already in an exclusive relationship with his son. There was no space for anyone else. He and the Little Prince had formed a very fluid family where the roles of father and mother and son were interpreted anew at each encounter. It was a strange merry-go-round of responsibilities and freedoms. It had all the noble sadness and joy of carousels, old music, worm-eaten wooden horses, and clanking mechanisms. But now the merry-go-round was slowing down.

All this he recounted to Carlini, who understood everything. He had now become the city's trendiest psychoanalyst and had an office resplendent with cream-colored leather furnishings.

And Carlini laughed at him. "Well, you've gotten yourself into real trouble now. You can't beat this. You're just a pill junkie like millions of your fellow men. You're dead now and the dead feel nothing. Joy and sorrow are just the same. If you really want to try and quit, though I don't see why you would, for you there is nothing but rehab. But you won't succeed. It's too late. The crime is complete. Drugs have taken your life from you."

"But everybody takes them. . ." said Morfeo.

"Do you know," asked Carlini from his high-quality leather throne, "what really separates one person from another, Morfeo? It's bigger, more essential, than the difference between men and women. Come on, you of all people must know what differentiates people in the modern world. . ."

"People who have children and people who don't?"

"I have none, and I live very well."

"Rich and poor?"

"Feh. That's no more essential than buying the right lottery ticket."

"Living and dead?"

"Hardly that. I, who dream and study dreams, meet them together all the time."

"The healthy and the sick?"

"Yes, exactly. That's the only real difference, whether you are healthy or sick. Do you want to be healthy again? Try it. Lock yourself in a Swiss clinic for six months, my friend, let them change your blood, spend those tens of thousands of Euros. But wait, you don't have a cent, do you, Morfeo? Farewell, my boy. Good luck. . . Enjoy your trip to Hell. . ."

So, almost by accident, Hell began.

It all started with an email. He was a young researcher, an absolute genius, and a friend of a friend. He was a frontier doctor, always in the midst of cholera and dengue, and he had a strong belief in the power of religious ceremonies and herbs. He was convinced he could treat Morfeo with the power of Nature.

But you can't treat someone by email. Technology is wonderful, but it's not enough.

For a while he was able to drop the dosage a quarter of tablet at a time. Then, suddenly, violently, insomnia set in. And like Death, the only way to face insomnia without fear is not to think about it. But insomnia became Morfeo's obsession.

It was an unequal struggle, herbs against fear. To make matters worse, the young genius was transferred even farther away, to somewhere in the Outback of Australia, and Morfeo lost his point of reference. The young genius had limited Internet access and his emails arrived every three, even four days. Morfeo continued the treatment, but things were getting worse. He ended up taking even more drugs and he counted his hours of sleep, one by one. He managed to hold it together during the day, but at the approach of night, panic would set in. His insomnia seemed invincible.

Morfeo had done ten years of psychoanalysis with a woman named Malvina, a cheerful psychoanalyst who was as doubtful as Carlini was snooty. This treatment had helped him get over a bad break up and had given him a period of stability with the Little Prince. But inside him, his dependence on drugs was always lurking. After the sessions stopped, he and Malvina, the psychocheerful, had become friends, so it wasn't possible to resume their professional relationship. All Morfeo could do was remember with fond nostalgia the many meetings of their younger selves. So Malvina gave him the name of a luminary of pharmacological psychiatry, Dr. Mirò.

He was serious and bearded. He talked about drugs, art, and chess, and looked like a Latin teacher. But then, one day, he said. "I'm leaving for two months, I'm going to sail across the Atlantic!" So Morfeo suffered a new abandonment, and there were new attempts with pills and sedatives, while insomnia continued to haunt him.

He then turned to Messeri, Carlini's rival and another one who had it all figured out. In his office, this time furnished in black leather, there was a painting by Bacon, probably fake, and photos of Freud. He had a secretary dressed in a peach business suit and a caiman leather sofa on which the city's elite described their dreams and talked about blow jobs.

Messeri had very different advice and even went so far as to mock Morfeo's previous doctors.

"Half the world sleeps badly," he laughed, "I don't sleep all that well myself. My advice to you is to try not to think about it."

So, having almost completely run through the list of available experts in the field of sleep, Morfeo found himself in a highly informed state of confusion.

He tried to carry on by himself, recalling, more or less, what one or the other of his often-contradictory experts had said, while mixing benzodiazepine and various herbs in a modern-day witch's cauldron. He was an open wound, every touch, every emotion felt like violence. He cried and did wonderful things with his musician friends, creating and suffering just like the artists he had admired. And people would tell him, "Your books have changed my life," but he couldn't change his own. Fear stalked him every night and he heard its approaching footsteps every afternoon.

During the month of August, while he had remained in Rome with his son who was studying for a difficult exam, he struggled on, tormented by abstinence, by dizziness, by confusion, and complex chess games made of improvised therapies. He was sleepless, lost, scared. Everyone he knew was concerned. He mixed Xanax and herbs, melatonin and herbal teas, and had a bag of drugs always with him. He was afraid to be alone. He spent his nights looking at his watch to see if he had slept and engaging in ritual preparations of drops and tablets on his nightstand.

On the rare occasions when he did sleep, it was pure joy, the joy of cheating Death. But he continued drugging himself ever more intensely. He tried to convince himself that he was fine but he had the gut-level fear of someone walking along the edge of a cliff. The bottomless void calls out to you.

He suffered, had brief flashes of hope, and then, suffered again.

Write it in large letters on the box. Write it. Write it.

He finally turned to a person whom he had never thought of consulting before. He was a friend, the psychiatrist Orio. Who knows why he had excluded him from his list? Perhaps he was too close. Perhaps he was too obvious a choice. Perhaps it was a trick of the Bad Angel. But, in the end, Morfeo decided to place himself entirely in his hands. Orio was cautious and calm. He was confident and poised. But most of all, he seemed to see a path forward that Morfeo could not see for himself.

So much time had been lost. By now, Morfeo was in a perpetual fog of confusion. He slurred his words. He staggered. He became obsessive. Before leaving the house, he double and triple checked his pockets: cell phone, two pairs of glasses, wallet, keys, drugs. He engaged in maniacal house cleaning, throwing away everything old, from wardrobes to small boxes, as if discarding these old things would also discard old habits and addictions and finally clear his head from the drugs that tormented him.

And the more he thought about what was happening to him, the more he shouted,

"Write this:

Take this drug for three months, then stop for three months.

Then you can start again, if it's really necessary.

Write it in huge letters.

Write it in 36 point font, not in tiny hieroglyphs that require a magnifying glass.

Preach it in schools.

Preach it to those who claim that 'everybody does it.'

And you, O Masters of Pharmaceuticals, you spend more on marketing and on selling drugs to your victims than you do on research and development, you bastards.

What you do is supposed to be sacred. It's supposed to be about healing. You should be taking it seriously, as seriously as death."

Then, one day, came a turning point. And all the lies, deceptions and evasions came to a sudden, explosive end.

His son marched up to him, looked him squarely in the eye and said, "Dad, I'm worried about you. You're going to die." Then he wept.

Morfeo collapsed. He decided instantly that he would go to a rehab clinic immediately. His son's tears were worth a million Internet searches, more convincing than the opinions of eminent psychiatrists, infinitely more powerful than his confidence in his own resources and his dreams of miraculous treatments. They were the traces of the Angels.

And so it was done. Morfeo would enter rehab. He chose the clinic where Elpis worked, the mysterious step-sister.

He cried for a long time after his decision. He felt humiliated, abandoned, angry. But mostly, he felt terror at the thought of surrendering his autonomy and his freedom.

They arrived at six in the evening. Morfeo had just one suitcase. Packing that suitcase had been cruel, every object inside meant detachment, estrangement. The toothbrush would now be a sick man's toothbrush, the cheerful red checkered pajamas would be the sad pajamas of a sick man, even his books and notebooks would never be the same.

"Goodbye, goodbye!" said the books while leaving the others in his study.

So with one suitcase and two books in hand, he arrived, as if in a dream, at the gates of the infernal Paradise, the rehab clinic.

It was a very different Hell from those usually depicted in paintings: a tall white building, with ugly statues in the park surrounding it.

A luxury hotel, more than a clinic. He passed through the doors, crying like a condemned criminal. Where's your courage, Morfeo?

Where was the road, the gate, the hope?

And then Morfeo felt her presence, a gentle breath of air from unfurled wings. He turned and saw her standing behind him. She had a flower in her hand and wore white, heeled shoes.

She was a Bad Angel, but she wasn't bad any longer, and, perhaps, not even an angel. She was the mysterious girl, Elpis, but no longer a girl. She had become very beautiful, and possessed Diangela's fire and Angedia's dark melancholy. She was indefinable. She was woman. She was man. She was a creature unto herself. Her wings were all colors and none.

She said, "I'm Elpis, sister, daughter, mother. I am your son. I am your fear. While you are here, I will never leave you."

Room 412

Elpis worked in the pediatric ward.

Morfeo found Elpis elusive, as if he were viewing her reflection in a pool of clear water. Sharp and focused when the pool was calm, but eerie and changing when the water was agitated. She was much younger than he, but somehow gave the impression she had lived much longer. She was slender and had a childish voice but strong hands.

She had a presence about her that no one could help but notice. When she walked by, there was the sound of the rustle of invisible wings just beyond the edge of hearing.

They passed a long hallway, a patient purgatory. Some were in their pajamas. Others were followed by wheeled IV drips like servant robots. Some were surrounded by noisy relatives, others silently alone. There was a crowd of people sitting on chairs and nervously pawing the ground outside the offices of various specialists. Each had an appointment and each had waited for minutes that stretched into hours and centuries. They waited for the magic words, for the vial, the elixir, the formula, the medical blessing that would wipe away their anxieties:

'This will cure you.'

"I'll take you straight up to your room," said Elpis. "You're lucky. I was able to get you in right away. People usually have to wait at least three months to get a bed here. But there was a cancellation and I've gotten you a spot in one of our shared rooms."

"But I would have preferred. . ."

"I know, Morfeo. I'm sure you would. I can see it in your eyes, but the single rooms are all taken. Even my power has limits," she said with an ironic smile.

Then she approached a desk, where a young, nervous, red-haired woman was chewing a ballpoint pen and fending off people's complaints.

"Velia," Elpis said, "this patient has a reservation for Room 412. Is it OK if I take him up right away?"

"Of course, Doctor," said the red-haired woman, after briefly consulting a register. "Let me call ahead and let them know you're on your way. But I'll need him later so I can finish checking him in."

"Thanks Velia, you're very kind," Elpis said, stroking her with the feather of her smile.

They entered a large, silent elevator that appeared to be taking him up to the fourth floor. But Morfeo knew that it was, in reality, sinking deep into the earth's crust.

When he left the elevator, Morfeo kept his head down and shuffled along the corridor staring at his shoes. He was already a patient, strangers could now tell simply by looking at his face. As he dragged his suitcase toward his own medical purgatory, he felt ten years older.

"I understand your discomfort, Morfeo," Elpis told him while waiting outside the closed door for the nurses to make the bed, "but look at it like this:

"You never walked in and you'll never walk out.

"Very few people comprehend that this hospital is the world and the world is a huge hospital. It's not something people want to accept, but it's true.

"All of us want healing. All of us try to avoid suffering, to escape Death one more time, to somehow make a difference, to matter.

"Those who are rich fool themselves into believing that healing is for sale. They buy every department head, every drug, every privilege, every comfort. They'll reserve luxurious rooms, lie down on comfortable beds. They fool themselves into believing this brings them safety, that no disease, no virus can enter, and that, if it does, it will be immediately hunted down and killed. That pain itself is fenced out. They are always disappointed. They, too, will suffer. There is no amount of money that can buy healing from the world.

"The poor man, instead, must endure humiliation. He'll believe himself treated unfairly and ask himself why bad luck always follows him. There is no space for him. He's ignored, ejected. He can't afford the hospital. The door is closed. But then the door opens and the coffin of a rich man is ushered out. A brief satisfaction, but the pain is still out there, waiting patiently.

"Yes, Morfeo, you already have a glimmer of the truth. As you'll learn, a hospital is a holy place and its acolytes should be an example to all. Good doctors are soldier-priests fighting to the last of their strength and the end of their life. But few are like this. Most think only about what they're going to do when the day is over and they can walk away from the battle. They have a wife, children, waiting for them, a house with a number on the door, just like a hospital room, their home, their shelter. They are only human. Humans treating humans.

The hospital is a microcosm of the medical industry. They're really no different. Most of the companies are out for what they can get. The welfare of the suffering isn't important. All that matters is making money. The medical industry is the world's third most successful, after oil and arms. Don't you feel proud to be a part of that?

"We are all cheating Death, and all doomed. The great white clinic of the world, floating in the universe, has just one fate in store for you, whether you believe in God or in a scalpel or in sleeping pills."

Elpis gestured with her white wing, pointing toward the door.

"Now, go inside. If, even in your sorrow, you can find a drop of solace to share with the others, do it. Or complain. Or cry out that it's unfair. Envy every person that in your heart you believe lives better than you. Tremble before each test, each symptom, each shrouded corpse as it's carried away. It is your choice.

"You fear the world of the hospital because it's filled with the temporarily living, but the hospital *is* the world and it's no different. Do you fear the world? Eventually, you will heal and you will leave. Do you have faith in me?

"No, Morfeo. To leave this world is merely to enter another. It's a rotating door that people of faith believe in, even though a black wing of doubt torments them every moment of their momentary life.

"I'll be by your side. But fear the deadly wind of my black wings. Perhaps, sooner or later, it will sweep you away. Perhaps I'll abandon you, or perhaps I'm lying to you.

"Do you have faith in me, Morfeo?"

With an enigmatic smile, Elpis disappeared with a clap of her wings and the door of Room 412 opened. Morfeo went in.

Let's meet the inhabitants of Room 412.

In the first bed on the left, asleep, there was Roby, a nineteen-year-old addicted to amphetamines and ecstasy.

On his bedside table, cookies, stacks of newspapers, manga, and a sketchbook in which he constantly drew hideous, menacing figures drawn from his stormy world. On occasion, these were self-portraits. From the sheets wafted a musky, animal odor.

And in the second bed on the left, near the window. . . Yes, it was really him, the inimitable Gaddo, freethinker, chronic alcoholic, and freedom fighter. He welcomed Morfeo with a shout of joy.

"It's really you! When I heard that someone by the name of Morfeo would be checking in, I asked myself, 'Is it possible there are two people with a name like that?' Welcome, my artistic friend! I wish I had some absinthe for you, but all I have on hand at the moment is a bit of cough syrup. Come on, Morfeo, we can do our dying together!"

On his bedside table, piles of political books, newspapers, all awash in the reek of a lion's cage with a hint of old cellar.

On the right, under the window, something wrapped in blankets, a two-hundred-year-old man in striped prison pajamas with a face like a skeleton's.

Nonetheless, on his bedside table there were piles of baked goods, chocolates, soft drinks, pieces of old cheese, and herbal teas. More than enough food, it appeared, for another hundred years.

The old man had white eyes and a lovely name, Narciso. They kept him there because he had been the gardener of Villa Poiana, centuries before. But he didn't suffer from any particular disease. Or rather, he had all of them condensed into one: decrepitude. Despite this, he stubbornly refused to vacate his bed even though thirty people were on a waiting list for his spot.

Morfeo chose not to dwell on who he himself had bumped off the waiting list, but now the room was full and the race was on. Who would be the first to heal? Who would be the first to die? Would it be Morfeo the drug addict? Gaddo the Bad Angel? Young Roby Rohypnol? Narciso the Dinosaur?

That evening, Elpis returned bearing gifts.

This was not her ward. She took care of children who would eventually become old and sick and graduate to other floors. But she was a constant presence throughout the hospital and hope trailed behind her like a lingering perfume.

To Gadariel, she brought a copy of *Moby Dick*.

"Gaddo, this is for you who were with me at the Battle of The Broken Wings, for you, who are terrible, as every Angel. Hermann Melville wrote one of the masterpieces of world literature, and yet, no one noticed, at least not while he lived. My wish for you is that your whale, the revolution for which you have fought, may triumph after your death. May it give you posthumous satisfaction. If you believe in our friend God, you'll see it from Heaven above. If you don't, that bright day will still come. Workers of the world will carry your name on their lips. 'Gaddo is with us,' they will sing. And be good. I almost killed myself getting you in here."

"Ha! And I shall succeed! You're a real bastard and a true friend, Elpis. It was an honor serving with you."

Elpis smiled. The Dinosaur, who always pretended that he never saw anything, opened one eye.

"This flower is for you, Narciso. Only among flowers were you happy. You hated people. You were a loner, perverse and greedy. But you created the most beautiful flowers, and so, the world is a better place."

"And what did I get for it?" sputtered the old man.

"The seeds that you planted will flower down through the ages. You are forever, old Dinosaur. Happy?"

"No. But it's a beautiful flower, a *Viola Biflora*."

"I'm pleased you like it."

"For you, Roby Rohypnol, I have many choices. I brought you some pencils to draw. And something else. You only appreciate musicians who died young. Well, for you I have a transistor radio. It plays duets by the living and the dead."

"Excellent! I'll play it all night and keep everybody awake."

"That you will not. I have brought you headphones, too. Roby, I know you live for suffering and curses, and that you believe this is what earns you the attention of the world. But beware. The world rejects those who suffer too much. They end their days alone."

"But that is the path of genius. The world always hates those who are different, who refuse to be like everyone else."

"Consider well, Roby. Would Van Gogh have traded one of his paintings for a day of joy?"

"I don't understand. . ."

"Listen closely and maybe you will. Morfeo, for you, a notebook. Write about all the good things you've experienced in life and about all your

86

experiences here. Imagine this notebook is your legacy and that someone will find it and read it long after you're gone. Seek the light, Morfeo. Find beauty in even the most sordid places.

Remember that blonde girl at your birthday dinner, many years ago? Well, I had fallen a bit in love with you. It gave me pleasant dreams. Now, I will return the favor so fall in love a little bit with me. And if you should, one day, escape from this place, go to Van Gogh and say, 'Here's money for a box of colored chalk and a bottle of good wine. Be happy today, don't paint the Sunflowers. In the museum, there will be a void on the wall. Billionaires will have one less thing to bid on at auctions. But there will be a day of happiness, wine and colors on the sidewalk. The colors will wash away in the rain. But that day, that wonderful day when the masterpiece wasn't painted and the painter was happy, will remain forever."

"I'll remember," said Morfeo, "However I leave this place, I'll remember."

"All right, my Angels, now it's time to sleep. The shades of night are coming, and I know that you fear the darkness. In this room that you now occupy, it can get very dark indeed. At night, not even the moon can be seen from your window."

A bell rang. Elpis stood in the middle of the room, like a statue, as the ward lights faded around her.

She returned to her office and sat at her desk with the lights out, staring into the distance.

And she saw. Narciso sleeps for just an hour, and then squirms, awake. He has a headache, and he soils himself. Roby gets up in the darkness and sneaks out of the room to try and steal drugs from the dispensary. Gaddo is half awake, alternating between screams and nightmares, remembering the past and when they kept him tied to his bed for six days. Morfeo can see no way out. The wind of sleep blows counterclockwise, it brings him confusion during the day and no peace at night. Shall we all flutter our wings together and make the Universe turn clockwise? But what is an hour or a night compared to the Universe?

Now Elpis had black wings, like a raven, and she closed them to sleep.

"Goodnight. I wish you all a sweet, good night," she laughed.

The Night

It wasn't a quiet night. The Dinosaur snored and farted, an orchestra of malevolent pipers. But sometime around three in the morning, he had an asthma attack and they carted him off to the intensive care unit. Roby, who had been breaking into a drug locker when the attack began, got caught stealing some liquid Valium and managed to drink quite a lot of it before they could wrestle it away from him. He sank into a deep sleep, like a baby after a bottle.

Gaddo screamed in his sleep. In his nightmares, he threw himself and his sword at the Archangel Michael.

"Look at humanity. Look at them! See how they suffer! How can you stay with Him? How can you defend this misery?

Which of us is the traitor? You can do more, much more!"

"A drop, a single drop. . ." answered the Archangel. "The world is an admixture with a single drop more of Good than Evil. You must cultivate that drop, think only of that drop. That is your mission, to be the source, to make that drop come from you. . . and obey!"

"A single drop. Look at the world. Can't you see? A single drop is not enough!" shouted Gadariel, amid the clashing of ethereal swords.

His bed shook and trembled, as if lashed by storms and earthquakes.

Morfeo cried. He just cried, that's all. And those tears were everything. A pure, agonized, clear cry, incorporeal and alone, infinite solitude. And yet, as the eons passed, there was, for an instant, the face of someone he loved and the thought that, at that moment, that someone did not suffer as he did.

Two days later, the Dinosaur still hadn't returned to the room and his bed. After his asthma attack he had left the intensive care unit and taken a walk through the freezing grounds to see his favorite trees. There, he caught pneumonia and was permanently moved to the ICU. Someone came and cleared his bedside table, removing the cookies, dirty pajamas, and the handkerchief he had used to wipe away his sweat.

Within minutes, his bed was ready for another patient.

His replacement was just a boy, Meo, who had lost half his foot after a motorcycle accident. He was in pain, but perfectly sanguine. Even his complaining held a note of hope that was unbearable for the other patients who had forgotten that such a thing existed.

For Morfeo, days of IV drips, sleepiness, and boredom began. Days of running up and down the stairs, to awaken his legs from their numbness. At night, he had a button with which he could summon the nurses. They would come and dispense a little sleep out of a needle or a pill.

People came to visit him, so many people. Of course, Morfeo knew he should be pleased but these visits made him feel even worse.

The Dinosaur was more fortunate than Morfeo and hardly ever received visitors. Only one of the nurses, a nice, cheerful Moroccan woman named Fatima, had ever paid him any attention at all. She would come to change his clothes and reprimand him as if he were a child. Fatima took an interest in everybody and everything, even in Morfeo's books and Roby's disturbed drawings. She talked with Gaddo about politics which frequently became arguing and bickering, but they always ended up laughing as well.

For the new patient, Meo, his sojourn in Room 412 was not a hardship. He already knew that he would be discharged after only three days. He was always quiet, and seldom moved once he had found a position that would minimize the pain in his half-missing foot. He drank water constantly and had a bladder of steel.

Meo was the only one who really had hope so, of course, Roby hated him immediately.

"I know how you got in here; you're the grandson of a surgeon. You've had an easy life. You grew up in the lap of luxury, not in a neighborhood like mine. You didn't see your father come home drunk and jobless. You didn't see your mother run off with another man. You had your beautiful motorcycle. Even your accident was lucky. You hurt your foot. So what? A scratch! If it had been me I bet I would have had my head cracked open like a melon. When you get out of here, your father will give you a car and you'll wreck it on the freeway, Anyway, I hope that's what will happen, pretty boy."

"Don't be like that," Meo responded, "we like the same music and I love the way you draw. . . when you get out of here, perhaps you can come visit me."

"Fuck you," Roby shouted, and cranked the volume on his radio up to eleven.

"Knock it off!" Gaddo snapped, "Or I'll smash your pathetic face, you little junkie. Why can't you let people die in peace? You only think of yourself, never of others even though they are suffering just as you are."

Having heard the shouting, two burly orderlies came in. They were not in a good mood.

"Hey! Knock it off! Keep it up and you'll both end up transferred to the psychiatric ward. Is that what you want?"

Meo started to cry. Roby immediately turned off the radio. Gadariel, instead, stared wordlessly at the two orderlies who felt a sudden, cold breeze that sent a chill down their spines and filled them with an unnamed fear. They left.

Morfeo, too, had been upset by the incident and escaped Room 412 to pace the corridors. Eventually, he came across Elpis staring out of a window on the fifth floor.

"You must leave this place," Elpis told him, "you'll soon be well enough to be treated at home. But it's not quite the right time, yet."

Morfeo said, "Soon? When? Help me. Be my Angel."

"An Angel is not always there, or an Angel wouldn't be an Angel. Their traces are ephemeral. It is their prerogative to sometimes come to your aid and to sometimes abandon you. Never knowing which it will be is the essence of divine intervention."

The next morning began in the most unexpected way. The Dinosaur came back to Room 412. He had run away from the intensive care unit, still trailing wires and a catheter. And he saw that his bed was now occupied.

He watered his plant and then jumped from the room's fourth floor window.

It made only a soft sound and there was no cry. The noise didn't begin until a few minutes later as the staff became aware of what had happened and began talking loudly.

Fatima, instead, said nothing when she entered the room, shaking her head with tears streaking her face. When she left, she took the plant with her.

Morfeo's Last Days

The bed that had been the Dinosaur's had just been redone when two women came in. One was an elegant, cheerful lady carrying a large shoulder bag. The other one was slightly harried, even worn out, and uncomfortable in the atmosphere of the hospital.

The cheerful and elegant woman was the Dinosaur's daughter. For years she had come to visit him every three or four months whether she needed to or not. As she rummaged through the cupboards stuffing her bag with her father's belongings, every gesture telegraphed relief and a firm determination to wrap things up as efficiently and as quickly as possible.

The worn-out woman was Meo's mother, who had come to pick him up.

She had driven all night to get there, and she was exhausted. She sat on the bed, her hand in her son's, and explained to him that a bit more time was needed to complete the paperwork and leave the hospital. She asked if his foot was hurting him in a sweet, feeble voice.

Soon, the two women began to commiserate with each other about bureaucratic complications and about how long they had to wait.

Eventually, Meo's mother helped her son to sit in the wheelchair, while the other woman continued her search through the cupboards.

As Meo passed Roby's bed, he asked, "Would you like me to leave you my comics?"

There was no irony in his offer, but to Roby, it was a slap in the face. He leapt out of the bed, tore Meo's crutches out of his hands and threw them against the wall shouting, "The golden child goes home to his mommy. Shove your comics up your ass. I don't need your pity. Go smash your other foot on a motorcycle or in Daddy's Porsche. And you, lady, there's no need to rummage through the cupboards anymore. There aren't any gold bars in there. Your father died poor and alone, like a miserable dog, you bitch. You're wasting your time. There's no inheritance here for you. Go to hell!"

"How dare you!" said the lady Dinosaur, full of resentment — she had gotten that, at least, from her father — "Who do you think you are?"

"Now, now, everyone please calm down," said Meo's mother, collecting his crutches, "This is a hospital."

"Holy shit! I hadn't noticed!" Roby Rohypnol sneered. He kicked the wheelchair, took the bag where the Dinosaur's belongings had been collected and threw it into the hallway.

Morfeo tried to intervene but Roby wasn't in the mood to listen.

"Get out of here!" he shouted, standing in the middle of the room in his underwear. "Enough of this fucking farce!"

Two orderlies came barreling through the door to confront Roby. One of them, called The Slab because, in both coloring and size, he resembled nothing so much as a side of beef, said:

"This time you're done, you pain in the ass. After you get out of the ICU, you're gonna be locked up in the psychiatric wing."

"No, wait!" said the other orderly, a decent, mustachioed little man nicknamed The Dwarf, "Just take it easy. Nobody needs to get hurt. Sit down, Roby, and let's talk."

But it was too late. Roby did not sit down and people were already getting hurt. The Slab had Roby's arm twisted behind his back and everyone was shouting.

Except for Gadariel. He flew across the room and, with a flutter of his wings, threw the bulky nurse against the wall with a resounding crash.

"Please, Gaddo, for God's sake," implored The Dwarf, "stop it, or you'll end up in the fucking psych ward, too. . ."

"I have spent more than half my life in a cage," roared Gaddo. "Here, there or somewhere else, what does it matter to an Angel? A cage is a cage."

That night in the hospital, silence reigned. The events of that cruel morning seemed a distant memory. Roby was no longer in Room 412, having been transferred to the psychiatric ward. Gaddo would follow him as soon as there was a bed available. But for the moment he slept, loaded up with enough tranquilizers to sedate a rhino.

So Morfeo was left alone, accompanied only by Gaddo's gentle snoring and two empty beds.

Morfeo stepped out of Room 412 and into the dark and silent corridor, lit only by dapples of light from the full moon. Strange. . . hadn't the moon been full when he entered this place? Had it been so long?

He walked for a long, long time, meeting no one. Eventually, he entered a strange ward he had never seen before even though, during the day, he had wandered every floor of the hospital for hours on end.

The ward was a great hall, almost a cathedral, with a huge window covered by a grate through which shone the lights of a city.

And Elpis stood by his side, with her white coat, her hair tousled. Next to her stood Gadariel, wearing a dark robe. Under the robe his wings, no longer broken and frayed, were majestic, iridescent.

"What are you two doing here?" Morfeo asked.

"What are *you* doing here?" Elpis replied, calmly.

"You should be in your bed sleeping," Gadariel said with a wry smile, "or perhaps you are."

"We are here to bid farewell," Elpis said in a low, mournful voice, "to bid farewell to Gadariel. Do you see those stars, just there? There we fought together in the Battle of the Broken Wings. We were defeated and scattered. But we continue to fight, to help human kind, here, in the world."

"And why should we bid farewell to Gadariel?"

"Gadariel has a bottle of rum hidden away in a place that only he knows," said Elpis. "He'll drink it all at once and that will be the end of him."

"Take it away from him," said Morfeo, "stop him. . ."

"I cannot," said Elpis. "I've explained this already. I'm an Angel and my destiny is to fly to those who call me, but not always. Sometimes, I must abandon and disappoint instead. Without evil, there is no good and it is only through disappointment that acts of grace become miraculous. Gaddo's comrades will come to celebrate the fall of the Dictator. I have no idea if this is true or not. Perhaps it's merely theater arranged by Gaddo's well-meaning friends. But it doesn't matter. Everyone will celebrate as if it were real, and Gaddo will say 'I have lived to see the Revolution. Now I can die happy. I deserve a good drink!'"

"But this is all so cruel. . .!"

"Then you have understood nothing, Morfeo," sighed Elpis, putting a wing over his shoulder. "You may not be cut out to be an Angel. I'll try to explain once more. Think of Moby Dick, Van Gogh and his sunflowers. Think of everything you've written, every sacrifice you've made. If we leave something behind us, be it joy for others, relief, a painting, a seed, a sacrifice, a moment of laughter, our existence has not been in vain.

"We were healers.

"Even the most evil of men, at least once in his lifetime, has done good. But there is a reckoning due from all of us. We Angels have given a drop more. Now we are lost. Heaven is not for us. But the reckoning and the drop remain."

"Elpis, enough. I'm frightened."

"You'll soon be leaving the hospital, Morfeo, and you'll be sent home. But I shall see you again."

The moon exploded in blinding whiteness. Morfeo awoke.

The Voice in the Dark

Three weeks after taking up residence in Room 412, Morfeo was discharged even though his prognosis was unclear. But Orio thought that Morfeo could be treated at home and that familiar surroundings would help his depression. Nobody had any better ideas and so it was done.

A nurse would visit him every night and help him sleep. He would have to take specific doses of specific drugs at specific times. Still chained to his disease, he was not free yet and that frightened him.

As he once again passed through the doors of the hospital and made his way to the car waiting to carry him off into the world, he was surprised to find that less than a month had passed. He would have guessed a decade. The world outside the hospital was familiar and yet not. A wind seemed to harry him, plucking at him. A wind that would blow him into the unknown should his feet leave the ground for even a moment. There was a dark roaring inside his head that made even the simplest acts of free will an agony.

He went back to his house and his study. He meticulously put all the things that had lived with him in the hospital back in their accustomed places. They all looked the same as they did before he had left, but he knew they were not. They, and he, had changed.

Thus began the period of the voice in the dark.

Every night, the ritual was always the same. A nurse would come to his home and briefly greet him. Then the nurse sat on the living room couch and Morfeo went into his bedroom and shut the door. Morfeo would go to sleep and when he awoke, he would call out. A disembodied voice would answer him and, in the darkness, a magical pill would appear in his hand, delivered by the nurse and administered as part of a complex therapy worked out in great detail by Orio.

At six in the morning, the nurse's shift would end and Morfeo was released from his purgatorial demi-consciousness. It was not sleep, precisely, but sleep broken down into its component parts and refashioned as something else, something that was neither sleep nor wakefulness.

But at six o'clock, Morfeo felt a momentary surge of relief: another night had passed. He would remain there, in the bed, for a while, lounging or even sleeping a little. For a moment, the pressure was off and he could do whatever he liked.

But soon, his day would start and the battle would resume. He had to find the balance, neither sleeping during the day, nor being unable to sleep at night, to stay active, yet unstressed. Every day was spent in preparation for the coming night just as every night was spent in preparation for the coming day. It was a chess game that Morfeo played against himself. And he was winning, he thought. He could feel his chain loosening, millimeter by millimeter, day by day. But he had to be patient, so patient. . .

His newfound clarity led to darkness as well as freedom. He had never seen so clearly before what had been taken from him and what he had thrown away.

He had forgotten, if he had ever understood, how much pain there was in his former life. All he wanted was to escape from his present one. He envied those who could dispose of their time as they wished, who had a schedule that changed day-by-day, who didn't spend their days thinking about sleep and Death. Of course, there were people living normal lives who were more depressed, sleepless, and unhappy than he was. Morfeo didn't care. He envied them. The hours, the days, did not proceed one into the next. They bent back upon themselves in an endless treadmill and there was no escape.

The traces of the Angels were no more than vapor, and a single thought or even a breath might be enough to make them vanish as if they had never been.

The first voice in the dark was that of a nurse named Rose.

Then there was another female nurse, then a male one, and so the first week of this disembodied dialogue passed.

One afternoon, while he was writing in his study in an attempt to keep his mind busy, news came of the death of Gadariel. It had happened exactly as Elpis had said it would. The Dictator had finally been overthrown by the people. Freedom had been declared and elections had been called. Late that night, an unruly gang of Gaddo's comrades-in-arms had broken into his room to bring him the news.

The orderlies had done their best to chase them out but they were hardened revolutionaries, not sick patients, so it wasn't easy. And in the midst of the mayhem, Gaddo danced on his bed, supremely happy, shouting, "At last! This time, I'll celebrate like there's no tomorrow!" When Gaddo's friends were finally removed from Room 412 and peace had been restored, Gaddo got hold of a large bottle of 160 proof rum he had hidden in a pair of old boots in the back of a closet. Later that night, when the nurse did her rounds, she found him on the floor in a coma with the empty bottle next to him. He died the next morning.

Morfeo went out to buy a newspaper and read all the details of Gadariel's death. He cried for a long time. Gaddo was well known in the city as a bad apple and people enjoyed thinking the worst of him. Newspaper editors were no exception.

Morfeo didn't go to the funeral. His days awaiting the nights were long, his walks around town uncertain. It was winter.

In the cold, his thoughts changed with every step.

Many of the people who had once come to visit him in the hospital had disappeared and he spent a great deal of his time alone. He now understood who was truly a part of his life and who wasn't. To visit a sick person in a hospital is a noble gesture. It is also a self-contained one. You know that you are just passing through, a word of comfort, a few minutes of sympathetic listening and you're out of there. Truly caring for the sick is a very different thing than visiting them and far more difficult.

The Little Prince remained by his side. It was not easy for either of them. There were problems. There was anger. There was also courage. And the Little Prince was not alone. A handful of other family members and friends also refused to desert him.

The others were dragged away by their lives, different lives that went in all directions. It was sad, but understandable, even predictable. Their involvement with Morfeo was reduced to a few hasty phone calls.

But Morfeo could not condemn them. He had not behaved all that differently with his parents or his own friends. With some, he had been a close companion until the end of pain. With others, he hadn't had even the courage to acknowledge it.

One night, a new nurse came to his home. She arrived late and said little. Morfeo thought it odd but he had his nightly ritual to perform and it could not be interrupted lest the Gods of Sleep be offended. So he left this strange new nurse sitting on the couch in the dark and retired to his room.

And then she spoke. "Good night," she called. "Tonight, I am here if you need me."

It was Elpis. Yes, for this one night, it would be Elpis who would steer his dreams.

"So you did come. . ."

"Well, there isn't much difference between an Angel and a nurse," laughed Elpis. "Or a body guard. So for tonight, I'll watch over you, my child, but do not ask me when I'll return."

"Yes, I know. I understand the rules now. You can see their traces, but if you try to touch them, they vanish into nothingness. Have I learned the lesson you set for me?"

"Perhaps you have," said a low, husky voice.

"Gadariel," said Morfeo, troubled, "why are you here?"

"Do you want to banish me from your dreams? I thought we were friends. Do you truly want to dream only of pleasant things? Is there room only for obedient, vindictive Angels, or do you welcome rebellious Angels as well? Do you want to offer up songs of praise or rain down curses? You're free to choose your own path during the day, why should your dreams not be free as well?"

"Gadariel, why did you kill yourself? Why did you do it?"

"If you go into battle, you expect to die. And the only way to cheat Death is not to try. We were as the stars in the heavens, that day in the depths of the centuries, and the sky was full of wings. The battle raged for a day and a night. We fought for a drop more, for just a drop more pity for mankind. But the others were more numerous and we were banished. And now we are called rebels, even devils. But though we were defeated, it is the winners who have lost. Their sphere is to sit in the heavens and welcome prayers while we live among men and suffer with them. Better to serve on earth than rule in heaven. Of God, we shall not speak."

As he drifted off, Morfeo smiled and said, "I don't know if this is a dream and I don't care. I'm glad you are still a part of my life, even if it is only in my imagination. I am a writer and so I shall write the last lines of our Book: *And so the accounts were finally settled and Morfeo, Elpis, and Gadariel were at peace because they left behind an extra drop. Their existence had not been in vain.*

"But there are always new Books and new stories to fill them.

"Elpis, you are real and when I have healed, we'll fall in love.

"Or I will fall in love and you won't, but I will still have passion in my life, even if it's unrequited.

"Gadariel, you will be a symbol of political struggle. Your example will be an inspiration and many will fight in your name, even Roby once he gets out of the psych ward.

"Or this is not just a fantasy. You really are Angels.

"Or I will heal and there will be more stories in my Book.

"There will be a new battle in the highest of heavens. But this time the rebellious Angels will win and there will be one more drop of pity for mankind.

"Two drops, instead of one.

"Pharmaceutical companies will be chaired by Angels and will spend ninety percent of their earnings on scientific research to discover medicines that are not addictive and miraculous elixirs that will allow everyone, rich or poor, to live for a hundred and twenty years with all their teeth and riding bicycles every day.

"On the other hand, since the average lifespan is already above average, perhaps we can settle, not for defeating old age, but giving it dignity.

"The young will have both hope and examples.

"Hospitals will be full of plants and flowers.

"And everyone will sleep well, or, if they don't, they'll paint sunflowers, fix that damn dripping faucet, and make conversation.

"Many relationships will flower among the sleepless.

"Whether or not you are Angels, I must thank you, because you have made me imagine something beyond fear, drugs, and pain."

"Correct, there are always new books and new stories," said Elpis. She opened the curtain of her wings and Gadariel disappeared behind them. "And now we have to accept Fate, my friend."

The Last Meeting

Morfeo began to sleep without the need of the voice in the dark. He still relied on the drugs, of course, protected by the same chemistry that had made him suffer so. And for the first few days on his own, he was afraid.

But then, things took a turn for the worse. The story ended suddenly and it ended badly. No more passion, unrequited or otherwise.

This is just one of the two wings, let's take a look at the other.

But then, his fear subsided, and his sleep was undisturbed. He needed to rely on the drugs less and less and, gradually, he returned to being free, the master of his own life. Then one evening, he returned to the stage for a musical performance with his son. In the midst of it, he suddenly realized that the black wing had passed. There would be a few more years of joy for him. This is what he was thinking in the dressing room of the theater when Elpis and Gadariel made their last appearance in the story.

"Well done, good show!" said Gaddo.

"The road has led you back to the traces of the Angels," said Elpis. "May you never lose them again. But you will."

"And when will that happen?"

"Who knows? Maybe it won't. Sometimes suffering is just a signpost on the road to happiness. Now, your happiness is fragile and you must keep it close. But it is a precious thing and you must share it with others."

"Will I see you again?"

"Perhaps," laughed Elpis. "Not tomorrow. And not where you expect. But we're never far away. Good night, once again."

Morfeo opened his eyes. He was eight years old or perhaps sixty. He was in his grandparents' house, in the chair under the window. It was snowing hard, and everybody was there: his mother, his father Giobbe, Grandmother Turtle, his grandfather sipping his broth noisily. There were only a few presents under the tree, but each one precious. And there, at the very top of the tree, was Elpis, her silver wings spread wide. The shutter creaked creepily.

Morfeo laughed, looking at the fire in the hearth and the sparks shooting up the chimney.

"Thank you, Angels. But don't be offended if my thanks go first to human kind and the joy people have given me. To my son, to my brothers and sisters, to my parents and friends, to Van Gogh and Melville, and to my creaky, battered writing desk. I am a rebellious Angel and I'll always choose humanity."

There was a tremendous splintering howl as the window shutter swayed and fell. Elpis leapt from her perch on the top of the tree and brushed Morfeo out of the way with her wings. It was just a fraction of an inch, but it was enough: the shutter barely grazed his head and crashed to the ground. Somewhere in the distance, Christmas bells rang.

The stories must go on.

THE END

Made in the USA
Las Vegas, NV
20 May 2023